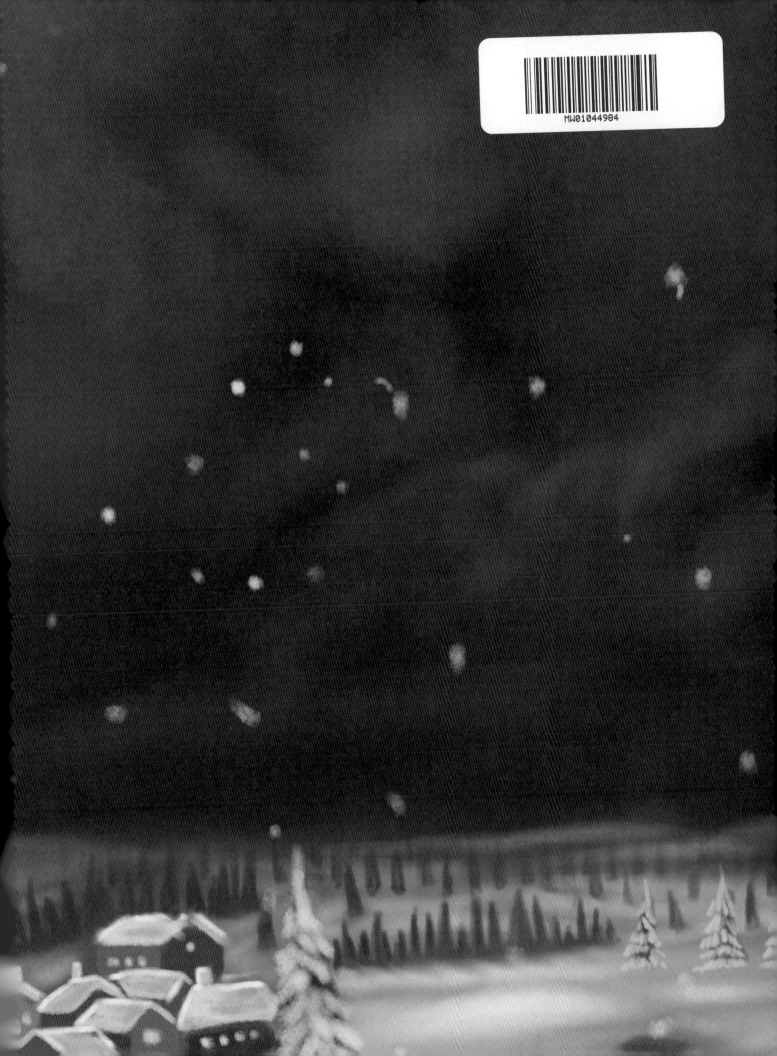

www.TaffyTalesPress.com
CHC-0912-0102
Made in China/Fabriqué en Chine

'Twas the Night Before Puck Drop

BY HARRY CAMINELLI
ILLUSTRATED BY
DHAMMA CAKKA

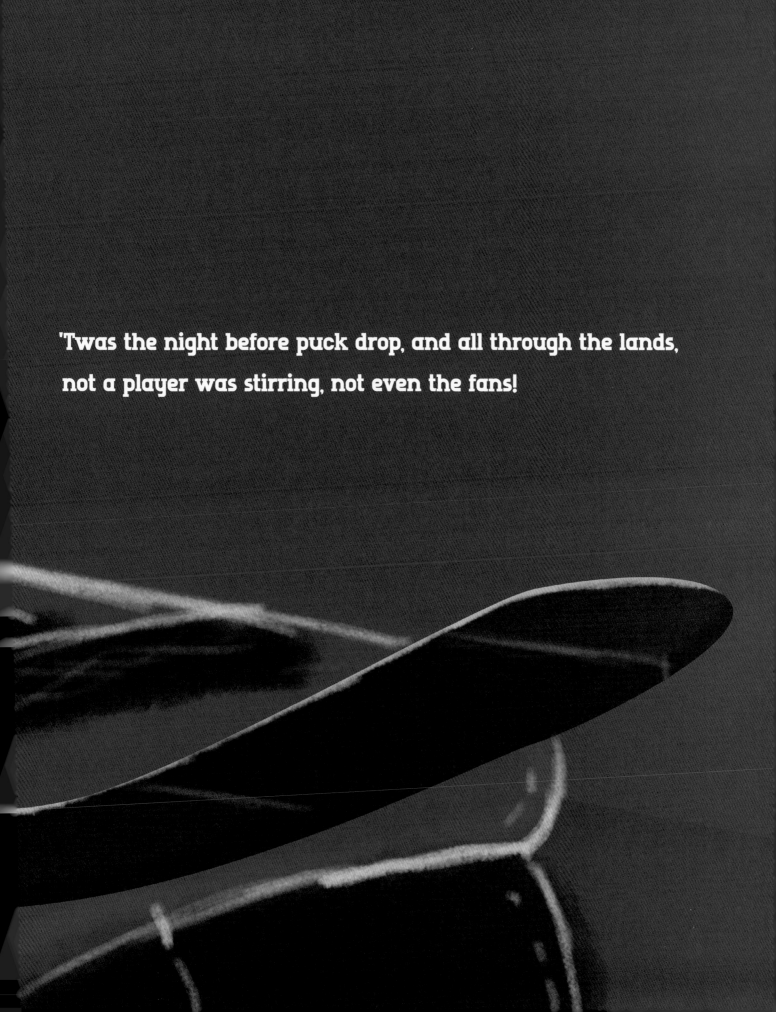

'Twas the night before puck drop, and all through the lands,
not a player was stirring, not even the fans!

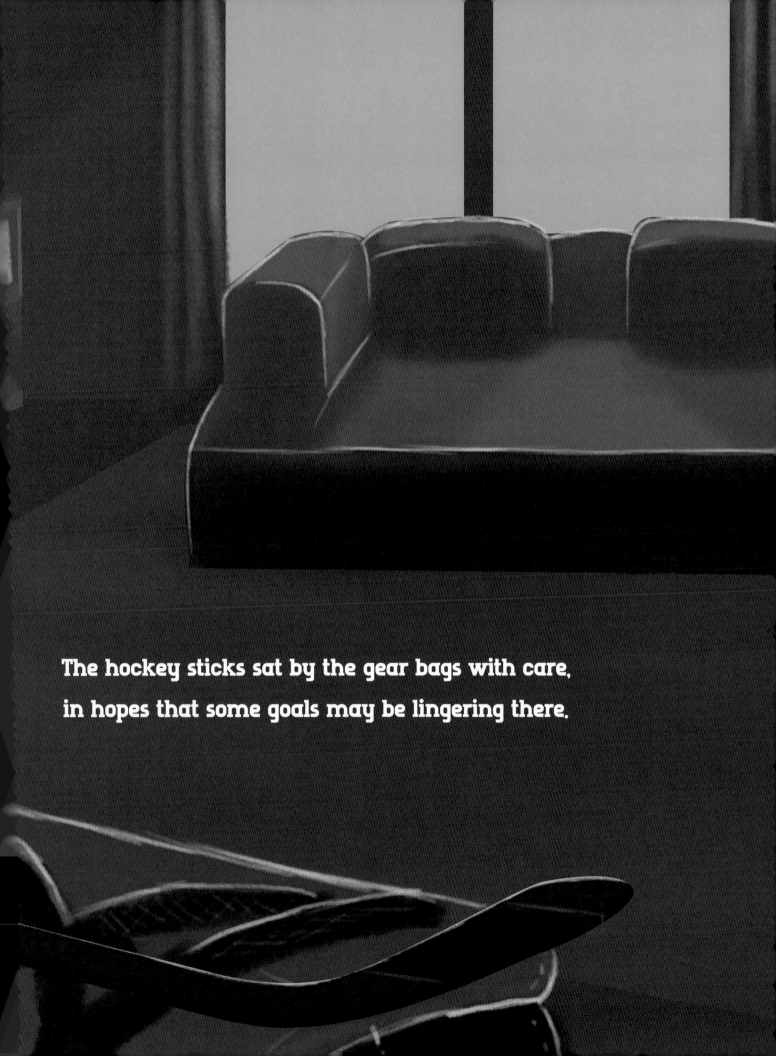

The hockey sticks sat by the gear bags with care,
in hopes that some goals may be lingering there.

The children were nestled all snug in their beds,
while visions of playoff games danced in their heads.
And Mama in her team shirt listed out every reason
why she was excited for this hockey season.

When out in the yard there arose such a noise.

I sprang from my bed to see if it was the boys.

I ran to the window while rubbing my eyes,

tore open the drapes, and got quite a surprise.

The moon cast a light on the new-fallen snow.

An area was cleared in my backyard below.

But it was more than a clearing, and I started to think

perhaps I am dreaming? Who made this sweet rink?

A player was skating, so lively and quick,

I knew in a moment it must be St. Nick.

More rapid than lightning his teammates all came.

And he whistled, and shouted, and called them by name:

"Hey, Bobby and Gordie! Come on, Sidney and Wayne!
Tell the crew to get down here! We're playing again!
Make your passes all crisp. Crash the net when you can.
Let's all hustle out there! And stay on your man!"

So down to the ice rink the players they flew,

with their bags full of gear—and a spare stick or two.

It took only moments for them all to get dressed.

Watching Nick skate end-to-end, they were mighty impressed.

Then the whole rink went quiet, and I heard a ref's whistle.

The puck hit the ice, and they were off like a missile.

I watched legends fly as they skated around.

Down the rink came Big Nick, on the puck like a hound!

He was dressed all in fur, from his head to his skates,
and he sauced up his passes; they went tape to tape.
His edges were sharp, and he'd hustle back.
He resembled the Great One when he went on the attack!

His eyes were so focused! His beard was so hairy!
His cheeks became rosy. His nose was a cherry!
His happiness was measured by the size of his smile,
and he said, "Gosh, I've missed this! Haven't played in a while!"

He played so intense, no doubt his mitts were quite smelly,

but his shot was a rocket, and he had a great celly.

His strides were real smooth when he flew 'round the ice.

As he kept up with my heroes, I thought, *wow, this is nice!*

He seemed happy and kind, a right jolly old elf,

and I cheered when he toe dragged and put one top shelf.

My kids watched in awe with a smile on their face.

Nick looked over and winked. He was loving this place.

He spoke not a word but went back to the game.
And the legends behind him? They all did the same.
And when the game ended, he gave them a look,
then a quick nod to go, and that's all it took.

He sprung to his sleigh, and they all piled in,
and laughed as they left saying, "Let's do this again!"

Then they yelled from the sleigh...

We came here for a reason: to say we love this game and wish you all a good season!

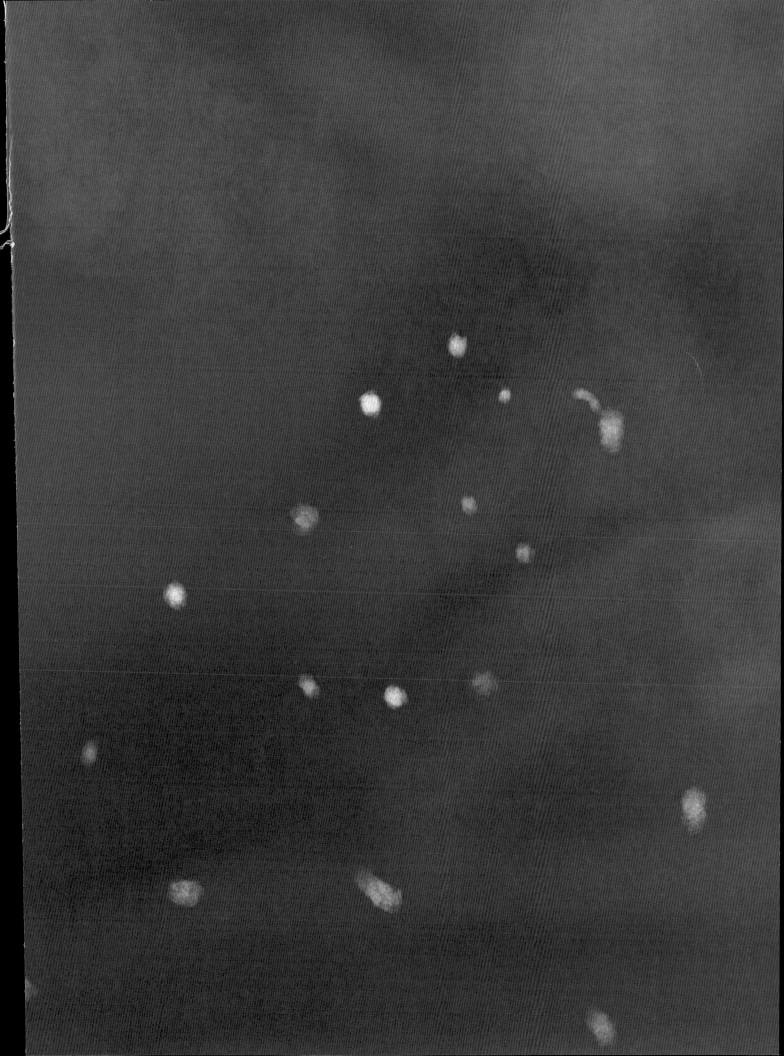